WHEN NO ONE IS WATCHING

Written by

Eileen Spinelli

Illustrated by

David A. Johnson

Eerdmans Books for Young Readers
Grand Rapids, Michigan • Cambridge, U.K.

When no one is watching,
I dance.

I leap and I spin and I prance
'round the room.

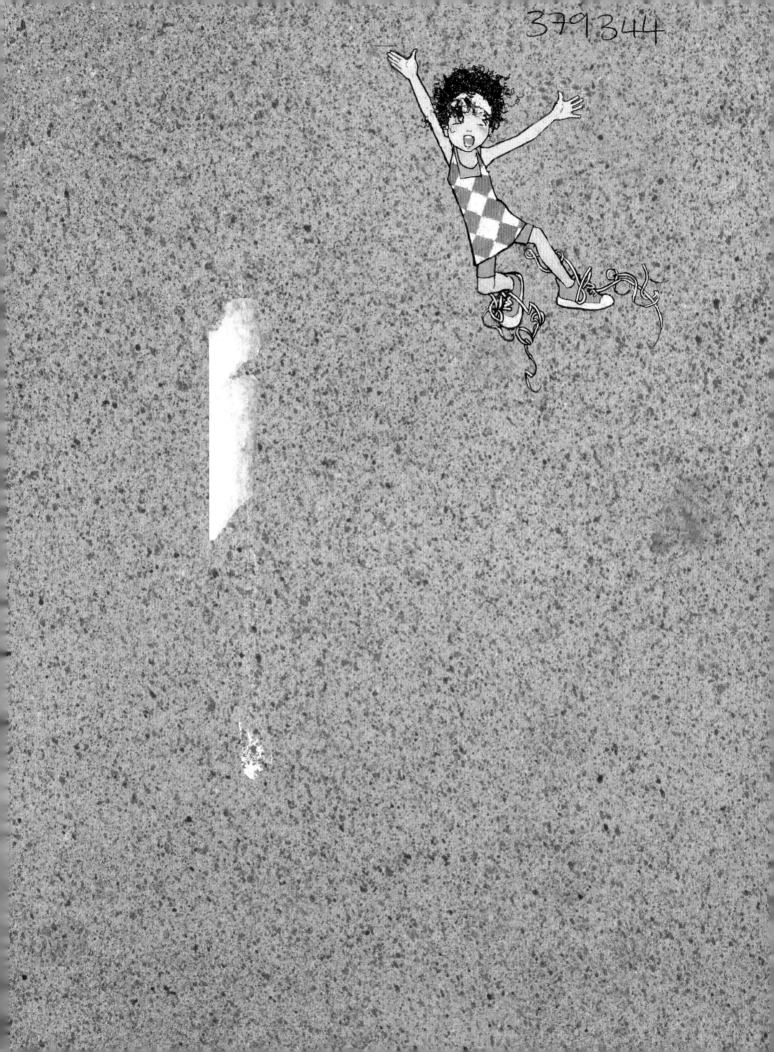

EILEEN SPINELLI is the author of over thirty-five picture books and novels, including *Jonah's Whale, Now It Is Summer, Do You Have a Dog?* (all Eerdmans), and *Someone Loves You, Mr. Hatch* (Simon & Schuster). Her book *Now It Is Winter* (Eerdmans) was named a Bank Street College Best Children's Book. Eileen lives in Pennsylvania. Visit her website at www.eileenspinelli.com.

DAVID A. JOHNSON is an accomplished editorial artist whose works have appeared in *The New Yorker, Harper's Magazine,* and *The Atlantic Monthly.* He has illustrated several children's books, including *Call Me Marianne* (Eerdmans), *Snow Sounds* (Houghton Mifflin), and *Abraham Lincoln* (Scholastic). David lives in Connecticut.

To Gail and Alyce, my writing friends.
— *E. S.*

To my art director, who got me through this book.
— *D. J.*

Text © 2013 Eileen Spinelli
Illustrations © 2013 David A. Johnson

Published in 2013 by
Eerdmans Books for Young Readers,
an imprint of Wm. B. Eerdmans Publishing Co.
2140 Oak Industrial Dr. NE
Grand Rapids, Michigan 49505
P.O. Box 163, Cambridge CB3 9PU U.K.

www.eerdmans.com/youngreaders

Manufactured at Tien Wah Press in Malaysia,
August 2012, first printing

13 14 15 16 17 18   9 8 7 6 5 4 3 2 1

Library of Congress
Cataloging-in-Publication Data

Spinelli, Eileen.
When no one is watching / by Eileen Spinelli;
illustrated by David Johnson.
p. cm.
Summary: When alone, a young girl enjoys dancing,
singing, growling, and cheering but when anyone other
than her best friend is watching, she is quiet and shy.
ISBN 978-0-8028-5303-5
[1. Stories in rhyme. 2. Bashfulness — Fiction.
3. Best friends — Fiction. 4. Friendship — Fiction.]
I. Johnson, David, 1951 Feb. 18- ill. II. Title.
PZ8.3.S759Whc 2013
[E] — dc23
2012025506

The illustrations were created using ink drawings,
watercolor, and digital manipulation
of a high resolution scan.
The display type was set in Funny Bone JF.
The text type was set in Impress BT.

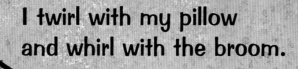

I twirl with my pillow
and whirl with the broom.

When no one is watching,
I dance.

But...

When everyone's watching,
I hide.

I hide like the cat
alongside
the big chair.

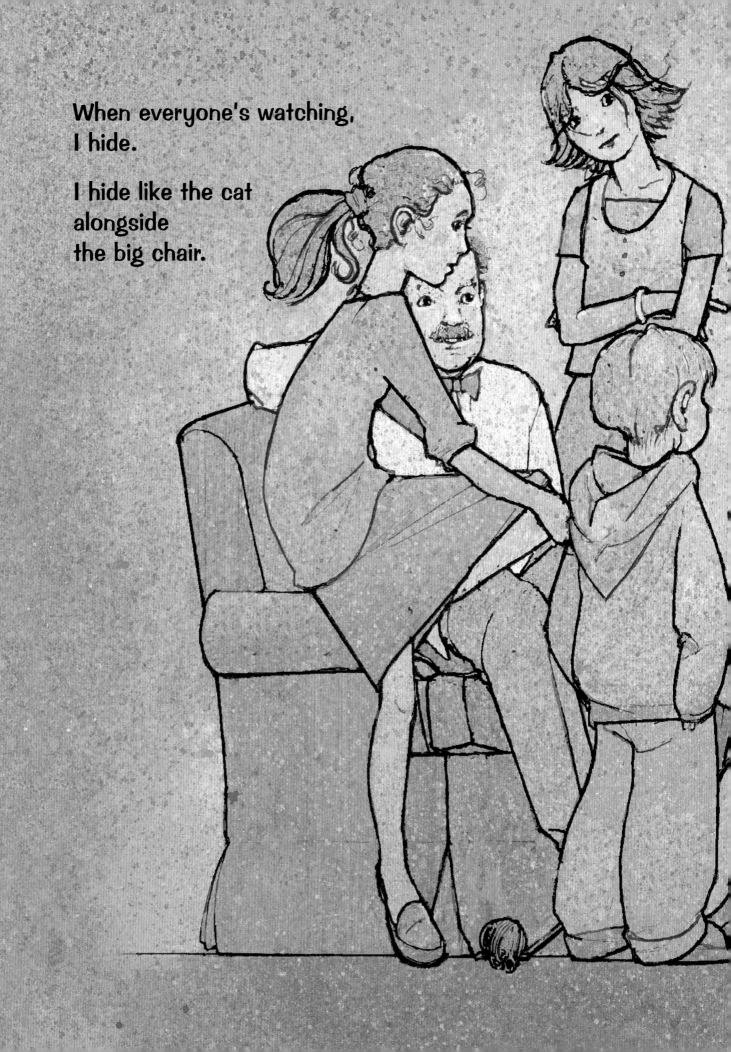

I scrunch myself down
and pretend I'm not there.

When everyone's watching,
I hide.

When no one is watching,
I'm brave.

I'm brave as a bear
in a cave
in the dark.

I tickle white shark.

I wrestle gorilla.

When no one is watching,
I'm brave.

But...

When everyone's watching,
I lean.

I lean like a bean
up against the old wall.
I don't catch the Frisbee.
I just let it fall.

When everyone's watching,
I lean.

When no one is watching,
I cheer.

I cheer for myself
as I race near the hoop.

I soar and I score
with a dunk and a whoop!

When no one is watching,
I cheer.

But...

When everyone's watching,
I pass.

I pass the b-ball
to my classmate Tamar.
Tamar makes the basket —
she's always the star.

When everyone's watching,
I pass.

When no one is watching,
I growl.

I growl and I grump
and I scowl
at the door.

I clump and I clomp
and I stomp on the floor.

When no one is watching,
I growl.

But...

When everyone's watching,
I hum.

I hum to myself
and I drum on my knee.

I wish I could buzz off
like some bumblebee.

When everyone's watching,
I hum.

When no one is watching,
I sing.

I sing like a bird
and I swing to the sky.

Who'd think that a tire
could take me so high?

When no one is watching,
I sing.

My best friend Loretta's shy too.
But oh we have fun
when we go to the zoo.
When the animals watch,
we just laugh.

We wave at the monkey.
We stretch like giraffe.

We neigh at the pony
and moo at the calf.

Together Loretta and I
are cozy and comfy.
We're no longer shy.

We splash in the summer
and read in the fall.
Together we don't care
who's watching at all.

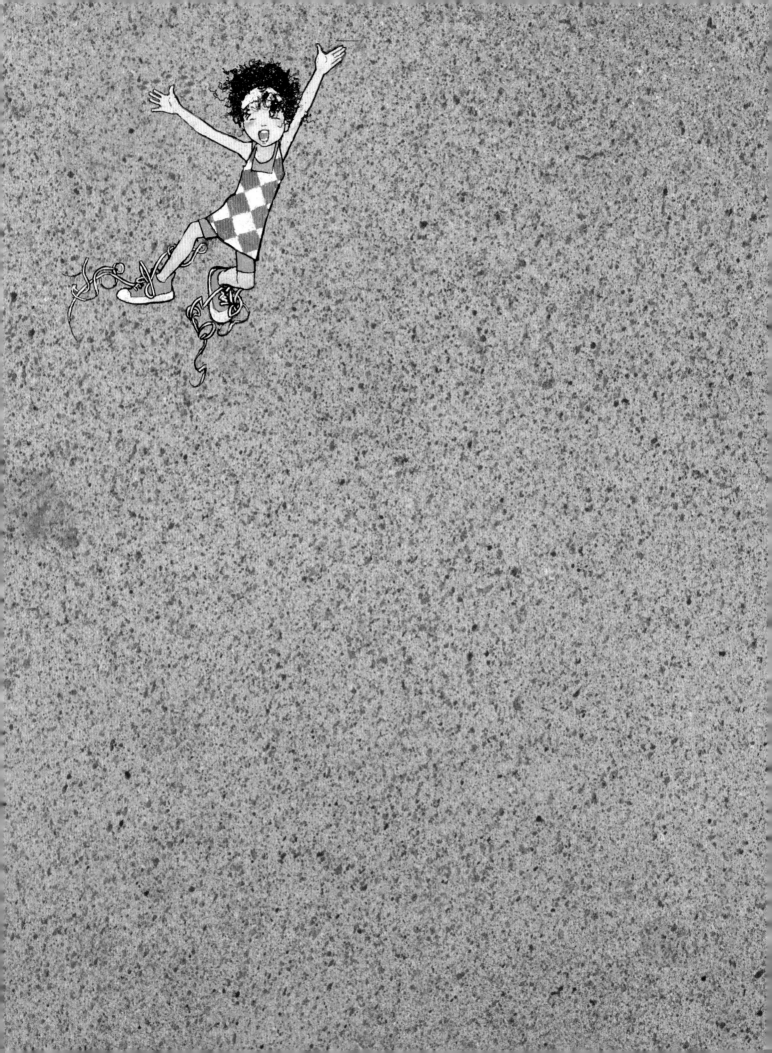

For Lydia, Abigail, and Margaret Huck
F. P. H.

For Emma Horne
J. F.

First published 2000 by Walker Books Ltd
87 Vauxhall Walk, London SE11 5HJ

2 4 6 8 10 9 7 5 3 1

Text © 2000 Florence Parry Heide
Illustrations © 2000 Jules Feiffer

This book has been typeset in Soupbone

Printed in the United States of America

British Library Cataloguing in Publication Data
A catalogue record for this book is available from the British Library.

ISBN 0-7445-7395-5